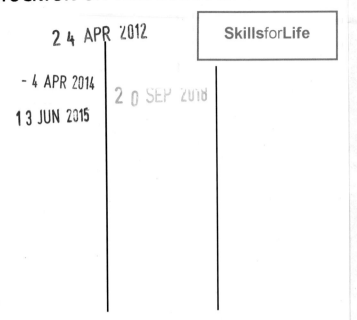
Piccadilly Press • London

D0544784

Phototypeset from author's disk by Textype.
Printed and bound in Hungary by Interpress
for the publishers Piccadilly Press Ltd.,
5 Castle Road, London NW1 8PR

A catalogue record for this book is available from
the British Library

ISBNs: 1 85340 503 5 (trade paperback)
1 85340 508 6 (hardback)

1 3 5 7 9 10 8 6 4 2

Terrance Dicks lives in North London. He has written many books
for Piccadilly Press including the CHRONICLES OF A COMPUTER
GAME ADDICT series, the HARVEY series and THE GOOD, THE BAD
AND THE GHASTLY series.

Cover design by Judith Robertson

PROLOGUE

Sobbing with fear, the man dashed headlong down the rocky path.

It was dark and the path was steep and uneven but he stumbled onwards with reckless speed, fleeing the unimaginable horror that pursued him.

Even as he ran, he could hardly believe what was happening.

It had moved – moved all by itself.

And now it was coming after him.

He reached the open ground at the end of the path, and headed for the road. The going was a little easier now.

He reached the edge of the road at last and stopped, gasping for breath.

His car was parked a little way down the road. If he could only reach it . . .

He was about to start running again when he sensed, rather than heard, the great mass moving behind him.

He turned and saw the towering shape out-lined against the night sky, the long alien face staring impassively down at him.

He screamed, just once, and then the thing that pursued him toppled forward, crushing him beneath its bulk . . .

Chapter One

SUMMONS

It's a long way to Easter Island.

You start off by flying to Schipol Airport in Amsterdam. Then you fly KLM from Amsterdam to Santiago, Chile.

That takes about fifteen hours.

Mind you, the journey is broken up by a compulsory stop-off for a few hours in Buenos Aires, Argentina, which isn't much fun either.

For one thing, you never get out of the airport.

For another, the presence of a number of sinister-looking uniformed characters makes you hope the Argentinians aren't still bearing a grudge about the Falklands War.

Dad was inclined to grumble about being kept hanging around in the passenger lounge.

He was all set to complain to one of the uniformed guards but I managed to stop him in time.

'Don't forget the first rule of survival in South

America,' I reminded him. 'Never annoy anyone wearing military uniform, dark glasses and a loaded machine-gun!'

Dad is Professor James Stirling, by the way.

I'm Matt Stirling.

Together we form the Department of Paranormal Studies, run by a big scientific foundation in America.

And why were we on our way to Easter Island?

It's a long story . . .

It had started on a rainy Monday morning a couple of days ago.

We were in the living-room of our top-floor flat in Hampstead.

Dad was grumbling as usual.

No one wanted to know about his scheme for restarting the space programme – his real passion and his job until funding was withdrawn and he had to take the position in the Department of Paranormal Studies.

Added to this, things had been quiet since our recent trip to Transylvania.

To make matters worse it had been raining for several days.

Dad stared gloomily out over the rain-lashed heath.

'I'm bored, Matthew, bored!' he announced.

'No intelligent person has any excuse for being bored,' I said.

Dad gave me his special withering glare. 'What pompous idiot said that?' he snarled.

'You did – the last time I said I was bored!'

I tried another approach. 'We must set up some interesting project for you,' I said. 'The Foundation pays you – us – to investigate the paranormal. If no specific assignment comes up, it's up to us to pick our own.'

'Such as?'

'There are hundreds to choose from,' I said airily.

'Name one!'

I'd been studying the strange, the weird, the unexplained, ever since we started this job. But, of course, as soon as I was directly challenged my mind went blank.

Suddenly a name popped into my head. I swear that it came from nowhere. Anyway, that's how it seemed at the time.

'Easter Island!' I said.

Dad looked at me as if I were mad. 'What?'

'Easter Island,' I repeated. 'Little rocky island in the South Pacific, miles from anywhere. Hundreds of huge statues of alien-looking figures, too big for the natives to have carved with primitive tools, too heavy for them to have moved . . .'

'I know all about Easter Island,' said Dad irritably.

I should have known – Dad knows all about everything.

'Thor Heyerdahl did a number of practical experiments there in the fifties,' he went on. 'He provided perfectly rational explanations for the creation and transportation of those statues.'

I struggled to remember my research. 'Not very convincing ones,' I said, just to be awkward.

Dad gave another of his scornful sniffs. 'I take it you prefer the theories of our friend Von Daniken? As I recall he maintained that the statues were constructed by shipwrecked alien astronauts who set them up as a signal to any passing spaceship!'

Erich Von Daniken was a Swiss hotelier who wrote a number of best-selling books with titles like *Chariots of the Gods* and *Return to the Stars*. He believed that all the wonders of the world, from the pyramids of Egypt to the temples of the South

8

American Incas, were the work of alien astronauts, who'd visited Earth at the dawn of time.

'Von Daniken was a believer,' I said. 'He
decided that statues *couldn't* have been made by
natives so they *must* have been made by aliens,
and looked for evidence to support his theory.'

'Precisely!' said Dad. 'Highly unscientific!'

'But don't you see?' I argued, 'Heyerdahl and
the others did the same thing only the other way
round. They decided that the natives *must* have
put up the statues and looked for evidence to
support *their* theories.'

'What's your point, Matthew?' asked Dad
wearily.

'Isn't it time somebody looked at the whole
thing with an open mind and drew conclusions
based solely on the evidence? That is the scientific method, isn't it?'

I'd got him there and he knew it!

For once Dad was stuck for an answer.

He glared at me for a moment. Then he was
saved by the bell – literally. It was the telephone,
ringing in his study.

He stalked off to answer it.

I heard him pick up the phone and snap,
'Yes? Ah, Ms Alexander . . .'

Immediately my interest perked up. Ms Alexander was the head of a mysterious intelligence agency. We'd worked with her several times before.

There was a moment or two of silence; then I heard Dad's voice rise in astonishment.

'What? Where? I see . . .'

More silence as Dad listened to the voice on the end of the phone. Then he said, 'Very well, then, three o'clock this afternoon.'

I heard him slam down the receiver and a few seconds later he marched back into the room.

He stood in the doorway for a moment, looking hard at me over his big horn-rimmed glasses.

'Well?' I said.

Dad rubbed a hand over his high bald dome.

'Sometimes, Matthew, I wonder if I should begin my investigations of the paranormal by studying you!'

'What's that supposed to mean?'

'That was Ms Alexander.'

'I gathered that much. What does she want?'

'She wants us to go to Easter Island.'

I have to admit I was pretty stunned.

Something like this had happened to me before.

Some time ago I'd started having nightmares about a haunted house called Borley Rectory.

Soon afterwards we'd been involved in an affair in which the rectory featured prominently.

Now it had happened again.

Was I plugged into some kind of supernatural Internet?

'Coincidence,' I said uneasily. 'Pure coincidence.'

'I hope so,' said Dad. 'Anyway, Ms Alexander has summoned us to a meeting this afternoon. She says she'll tell us all about it then.'

The meeting had taken place in a small but luxurious conference room in an anonymous building beside the Thames.

Ms Alexander hadn't been able to tell us much.

Apparently Easter Island is a province of Chile – which was news to me. Britain was anxious to improve relations with the newly democratic Chilean Government, especially after the unfortunate Pinochet affair.

Weird things were happening on Easter Island. The Chilean Government had turned to the British Government for help; the Government had passed the buck to the Intelligence Service and Intelligence had passed it on to us.

Not surprising, really. When it came to the weird and wonderful, they had nobody else to turn to.

After the usual greetings and reminiscences it was time to get down to business. Ms Alexander turned to her assistant.

'Will you take over the briefing please, James?'

Jim Wainwright is a large, tough and cheerful young man, a kind of real-life James Bond without the pretentiousness. He's the sort who prefers a pint of bitter and a pie to a vodka Martini, shaken but not stirred.

Wainwright studied the file in front of him.

'It concerns these giant statues . . . Apparently there are nearly a thousand of them. Nobody really knows how the natives managed to make them or to move them.'

I couldn't resist the opportunity to wind Dad up.

'If it was the natives . . .'

Wainwright looked baffled. 'Sorry?'

'There are other theories,' I said mysteriously.

Dad was beginning to get impatient.

'Easter Island has been the subject of study and speculation for many years. There are a variety of theories concerning the statues and their origins, some sensible, some fanciful in the extreme.' He gave me his withering glare.

I grinned back cheerfully. 'As you always say, it's important to keep an open mind!'

Ignoring the interruption, Dad went on. 'Since the business of your department is intelligence and not archaeology, what has Easter Island got to do with you – and us?'

Ms Alexander and Jim Wainwright looked at each other. Ms Alexander drew a deep breath. 'These statues,' she said. *'Moai*, I believe they're called . . .'

'What about them?' snapped Dad.

'They seem to be . . . on the move.'

This time it was Ms Alexander who got the glare.

'Moving? By themselves? Surely you can't be serious?'

'They're moving all right,' said Jim Wainwright. 'And now one of them's killed someone . . .'

Chapter Two

ARRIVAL

Ms Alexander gave us the facts – such as they were.

Apparently Easter Island had been seething for some time with rumours that the statues were on the move. Since there were so many of them, this was hard to prove or disprove.

According to Chilean Intelligence reports, the native islanders were mysteriously convinced that some great event was about to take place. There were mutterings about 'the return of the gods'.

'Easter Island – Rapanui, the natives call it – has been a province of Chile for over a hundred years,' said Jim Wainwright. 'There was some repression at first, but these days the administration seems to be pretty liberal. All Rapanui have full Chilean citizenship, and the Governor of the island is a Rapanui.'

Nevertheless, explained Wainwright, relations between native Rapanui and Chileans, who made up most of the island's civil servants and members of the armed forces, had always been just a bit edgy.

'The Chilean authorities feel they ought to do *something* about this statue business,' he said. 'But they don't want to provoke a riot, especially since Rapanui outnumber them by about two to one.'

What had brought things to a head was the death of Doctor Rankin, an English archaeologist, one of a party working on the island.

He was found crushed to death on a lonely road – beneath a giant statue. The nearest known site of any statue was half a kilometre away.

'The fact that the dead man was British led to the involvement of the British Government, and eventually to that of my department,' said Ms Alexander.

'And us!' I said.

Dad frowned. 'That's the bit that bothers me. Exactly what are we supposed to do?'

'Investigate this mysterious death, I suppose,' I said.

Ms Alexander nodded. 'Precisely! And, more importantly, discover what's behind it.'

I looked at Wainwright. 'You said something

about reports from Chilean Intelligence. Have they got agents out there?'

Jim Wainwright grinned. 'Don't miss much, do you, young Matthew? I asked about that, but they were pretty cagey. Eventually they admitted they'd been getting reports from an agent called Santera. They wouldn't say much about him – except that he'd give you his help if you needed it.'

'Let's hope he doesn't try,' said Dad. 'The last thing we want is some South American James Bond getting under our feet.'

'Santera is one of their top people,' said Ms Alexander. 'I worked with him myself once. He had quite a lot to do with the overthrow of the Pinochet dictatorship.' Just for a moment, her face seemed to soften. 'He was – quite impressive.'

I had a sudden picture of Ms Alexander sipping cocktails with some suave Latin lover under the South American moon.

Dismissing the unlikely thought, I said, 'Anything else we ought to know?'

'I don't think so,' said Wainwright. 'I'll give you a copy of the file.' He grinned. 'You can read it on the plane. There'll be plenty of time – it's a *very* long flight!'

That had been more or less it.

After a certain amount of humming and hawing and mutterings about being a scientist not a policeman, Dad had agreed to go. Largely, I suspected, because it beat staring out of the window at the rain.

Ms Alexander's department had operated with its usual efficiency, fixing us up with first-class travel and diplomatic passports. We also had official credentials, though we'd decided not to use them unless we had to.

'Much better to go out there as tourists,' said Dad.

'I'll have to let the Chilean Authorities know you're coming,' said Ms Alexander. 'But I'll request that they leave you alone unless you ask for help . . .'

So, here we were – hanging about in Buenos Aires airport on the way to Easter Island.

Air travel was all very well when you were actually *in* the air, I reflected. It was all the bits in between that seemed to take forever.

Suddenly I became aware of a big hairy shape looming over us.

I looked up and saw a very large man with a

very large beard. He wore a baggy tweed suit, a long flowing overcoat and a floppy hat, and looked like a sort of hairy, tweedy cloud.

He spoke to Dad.

'It's Professor Stirling, isn't it?'

There was a Scottish burr in his voice that turned Stirling into Stairling.

Dad's not all that sociable at the best of times and right now he was tired and even grumpier than usual.

'That's right. And you are?'

'Abernethy. Professor Andrew Abernethy. We met at the ecological conference in BA a few years ago.'

Dad roused himself to go through the motions. 'Yes, of course. How do you do?'

I coughed, and Dad glanced at me, remembering I was there. 'This is my son, Matthew.'

I did my best to make up for Dad's bad manners. 'How do you do, sir?' I said politely, and got up and shook hands.

Abernethy grabbed my hand in a huge, hairy paw. 'Verra pleased to meet you. This is a fine big lad you have here, Professor Stirling. I didn't know you had a son.'

I opened my mouth and then closed it again.

I'd *nearly* said, 'Neither did he until recently,' but managed to stop myself in time. It would have been tactless to say the least, and besides, it wasn't quite true.

Mum and Dad separated soon after I was born, and although Dad knew I was there, I doubt if he remembered it very often.

When Mum died in an accident her sister Ellen took me in. It wasn't till her husband retired and they both went to live in Spain that Dad found me on his hands again. By now I was nearly sixteen and six feet tall – very different from the baby he'd left behind.

He'd got the paranormal research job at about the same time, so he took over responsibility for my education – Dad has a whole string of degrees – and took me on as his assistant.

Since then we'd lived and worked together in an occasionally prickly partnership.

None of which was any concern of Abernethy's.

I got my hand back before he crushed it and he turned to Dad.

'And what brings you back to BA, Professor Stirling?'

'Nothing,' said Dad briefly. 'We're stopping

over on our way to Santiago.'

'And what's going on there? Another confer-ence?'

All these questions weren't doing Dad's temper any good. 'Not as far as I know,' he said shortly. 'We're travelling on to Easter Island.'

'Are you so? Now there's a coincidence. I'm bound there myself.'

I decided it was our turn to ask the questions.

'What takes you there, Professor Abernethy?'

'Work, laddie. I'm an archaeologist, and I have an expedition there. I went back to London to raise more finance but I'm having to rush back early.'

I put on an expression of innocent interest. 'Why was that?'

'There was a terrible accident. One of my team was killed by a falling statue.' He was still looking at Dad. 'And why are you going to Rapanui, Professor Stirling? Have you a project there yourself? It's hardly your field.'

Dad was clearly about to tell him to mind his own business, so I jumped in before he could speak.

'Nothing like that,' I said hurriedly. 'Just tourism. Things are a bit quiet in the space race just now, so Dad's improving my education with a world tour.'

I babbled out this nonsense as convincingly as I could, but Professor Abernethy still looked sceptical.

An announcement, first in Spanish, then English, crackled over the tannoy and Dad stood up.

'There's our plane at last . . .'

As we moved towards the gate Professor Abernethy said, 'If I don't see you on the plane, I don't doubt we'll run into each other on the island, Professor Stirling. Take care while you're there, won't you? There's a wee bit of unrest at the moment. Just stick to the usual tourist sights and you'll come to no harm.'

As we settled back in our seats for the second leg of the long flight, I said, 'Old Abernethy didn't seem overjoyed at having a fellow scientist joining him on the island.'

'All these archaeologists are paranoid,' said Dad dismissively. 'He's probably on the trail of the Easter Island equivalent of King Tutankhamen's tomb and he's afraid I'll find it first.'

'He's not entirely wrong, is he?' I said.

'What do you mean, Matthew?'

'Well, we are looking for some kind of secret on Easter Island. Maybe he's looking for it too.'

I could still hear Abernethy's parting words. 'Just stick to the usual tourist sights and you'll come to no harm.'

Somehow they'd sounded like a warning – or a threat . . .

We reached Santiago at last, and hung around in the airport some more, waiting for our flight to Easter Island.

I didn't see Professor Abernethy again until we were about to board the plane.

To my surprise, and relief, the plane was a full-sized jumbo jet. I suppose I'd been expecting some kind of wood and canvas biplane, or an ancient flying boat.

I said as much to Professor Abernethy who was standing behind us in the boarding line.

'We owe that to our American friends,' he said. 'They were worried that one of their space shuttles would splash down near the island, so they spent a fortune extending the airstrip in case they needed it for the rescue plane. Typical of the

Yanks, more money than sense. Still, it means we can travel in comfort.'

We made our way on to the plane and found our seats.

This was the last leg of our journey, a mere five hours flying-time. With fifteen hours flying behind us we soon dropped off to sleep.

I had confused dreams about giant stone figures toppling over to crush me . . .

One of them reached out and grabbed my shoulder and I woke up with a start . . .

'Wake up, Matthew,' said Dad. 'We're here!'

It was night by the time we arrived, and my first impression of Easter Island was of a warm, moist blackness, scented with tropical flowers. We staggered across the tarmac and into the air terminal, which wasn't much more than a large, brightly-lit hangar. There were the usual formalities, though I was too tired to take much in. As we stood around waiting for our luggage I caught a glimpse of Professor Abernethy being met by a tall, fair-haired young man and a small, dark-haired girl.

Not everyone had got off the plane. Dad said most passengers were travelling on to Tahiti and New Zealand.

However, there were enough Easter Island passengers to form a considerable scrum when the luggage finally arrived. There was no carousel, they just drove it in on one of those baggage-train things and dumped the lot in a pile, leaving you to sort it out for yourselves.

The situation was made even worse by the sudden arrival of a happy crowd of Easter Islanders, colourfully dressed in Hawaiian shirts. Some of them began throwing garlands of flowers round the dazed tourists' necks.

Others concentrated on making a grab for the tourists' luggage.

I guessed that this last lot must be hotel and taxi touts.

Dad waved away a particularly enthusiastic garland-hurler and looked at the heaving crowd with horror. I could see he wasn't going to be much help.

I was bracing myself to plunge into the fray when a voice in my ear said, '*Señor*? If you will be kind enough to describe your luggage, and that of the other distinguished gentleman?'

I turned and saw a small, slim, dark-skinned man in faded jeans and a ragged white T-shirt. His jet-black hair fell in a jagged fringe over bright brown eyes and he had a drooping moustache and a stubbly chin.

'Who are you?' I asked sleepily.

'I am Carlos, *señor*, at your service. Now, the luggage?'

For all I knew he might be the local bandit and luggage thief but I was so tired I welcomed any help I could get.

'Two brown leather suitcases,' I said. 'And a big, black canvas hold-all, all labelled Stirling.'

Carlos plunged into the fray and emerged minutes later with my hold-all over his shoulder and a suitcase in each hand.

I went to help him, but he shook his head. 'No problem, *señor*, I am small but I am very strong. Now, if you will do me the honour to follow me? My taxi is waiting.'

He marched off with our luggage and we followed him outside.

The 'taxi' was a big brown Land Rover, old and battered but well cared-for. Carlos put the baggage into the back, ushered us into the rear passenger seats, climbed behind the wheel and we zoomed away into the darkness.

'Your hotel, *señores*?' he asked.

I looked at Dad who yawned.

'I think it's called the Splendide.'

'The Splendide, naturally, where else?' said Carlos. 'The finest hotel on the island!'

We drove on into the darkness on the bumpy, unpaved roads.

'What made you pick on us, at the airport?' I asked.

'I have the eye,' said Carlos simply. 'I have education, me, I am from Santiago! On every flight there are passengers of distinction, those who will appreciate the service that only I, Carlos, can give. I meet them, I make myself known, we come to an arrangement . . . it is done!'

Dad gave a modest cough and said, 'Well, really . . .'

I could see he was flattered by being instantly recognisable as a man of distinction.

Myself, I wasn't so sure. Carlos would bear watching, I decided sleepily. But not tonight.

I was too tired to worry about anything tonight.

The Splendide, when we reached it, wasn't really all that splendid, just a collection of scattered bungalows round a single-storied main building.

But at least they seemed to be expecting us.

Very soon we were booked in and Carlos was carrying our luggage to a two-bedroomed bungalow.

Dad reached in his pocket for his supply of local currency, but Carlos waved the money away. 'The *señor* must not trouble himself with such trivialities when he is tired. We will talk tomorrow. I have the honour to wish you good night, *señores!*'

He bowed and disappeared into the darkness.

Dad and I said our goodnights and staggered off to bed.

I awoke to find sunlight streaming into the room. I looked round sleepily, and found myself on an old-fashioned bed in a simply furnished bedroom with whitewashed walls.

For a moment I wasn't quite sure where I was.

But I knew as soon as I climbed out of bed and went over to the window. The hotel was built on a cliff edge. I could hear and smell the sea.

From the skyline, very close to the hotel, three of Easter Island's giant statues, the *Moai*, were watching me. They stood on a rough stone platform on the edge of the cliff. They had long, sad faces, wide, almond-shaped eyes. Their backs were to the sea and for a moment it seemed they must have turned round to look at me.

Then I remembered reading that the *Moai* usually faced inland, gazing down at the villages under their protection.

I looked up at the statues.

They stared impassively down at me, massive alien shapes with something ominous about them.

It was almost as if they were threatening me, warning me to go away.

Well, we've reached Easter Island, I thought. What next?

I was soon to find out.

It was to prove more terrifying than anything I could possibly have imagined.

Chapter Three

THE SEARCH

My mystic communion with the *Moai* was broken by the sound of a rasping snore.

I went into the adjoining bedroom and woke up Dad.

We grunted good mornings at each other, got washed and dressed and went over to the main building for breakfast.

The breakfast, like the breakfast-room, reminded me of a modest sea-side hotel. A bright, sunny room, a scattering of tables and waitresses serving porridge and bacon and eggs.

Dad sipped his coffee like a man expecting the worst but the coffee, like the food, was surprisingly good.

'Well, what now?' he said, when he'd cleaned his plate.

We were still both feeling a bit jet-lagged, and it seemed hard to make any decisions.

'We're supposed to be tourists, so we'd better

act like it,' I said. 'We can take a trip round the island. There are coaches outside, and I expect the hotel arranges tours.'

Dad glanced round at our fellow guests, mostly elderly, mostly prosperous-looking.

'A day on a coach with this lot, listening to some guide?'

'I see what you mean.'

'What about that nice little chap who turned up last night?' said Dad thoughtfully. 'Apart from anything else, we still owe him for the trip from the airport. We ought to try and find him.'

I looked out of the window and grinned. 'That shouldn't be too difficult.'

A battered old brown Land Rover, now polished and gleaming, was just drawing up outside the hotel.

Carlos jumped out and stood beside it. He was wearing the same sort of clothes as yesterday, with the addition of a battered straw hat and a crumpled linen jacket.

He saw me looking at him through the big breakfast-room window, swept off the hat and bowed low.

I waved back, and Carlos replaced his hat, folded his arms and leaned against the Land

Rover, like someone with all the time in the world.

I turned back to Dad.

'It won't be any problem finding Carlos. I don't think we could lose him if we tried!'

When we came out of the hotel, Carlos was being yelled at by a burly, crew-cut tourist with a loud voice and an even louder Hawaiian shirt.

'Don't you understand plain English, boy? I'm hiring you and your heap for the day. Here, you can name your own price!'

He produced a wad of dollars and waved them at Carlos.

'I am sorry, *señor*, it is not possible,' said Carlos with quiet dignity. 'I am already engaged in the service of the most distinguished professor.'

He turned to Dad as we approached. 'Is that not so, professor?'

'It most certainly is,' said Dad.

He gave the tourist his most freezing glare. 'Do you mind, sir? This is my car and my driver!'

The tourist retreated, red-faced and muttering.

Dad turned back to Carlos. 'You really must let me settle up, Carlos. Here you are, turning away good money, and we're already in your debt.'

Carlos waved the offer aside. 'Do not concern

yourself, professor. We will agree a daily rate, and you pay me at the end of your stay.' He looked at the retreating tourist. 'As for that one! No amount of money can compensate for serving such a pig!'

He ushered us into the Land Rover and we drove away.

'First I give you the general tour of the island,' said Carlos over his shoulder. 'The big picture, as you say! Then you tell me the places you wish to visit, and it will be my pleasure to drive you there. Later, if you wish to eat, or to drink or to shop, I know all the best establishments . . .'

We set off on our grand tour of Easter Island.

Imagine a rocky chunk of Cornwall dropped miles from anywhere in the vastness of the South Pacific, five thousand kilometres from anywhere. The island is triangular and there's an extinct volcano at each corner. The south coast, the longest, is only twenty-two kilometres long.

On that first day Carlos drove us over most of the island, across a bare landscape with low, rolling hills. We saw volcanic craters that had turned into murky, reedy lakes.

And we saw more of the great stone statues, the *Moai*.

'There are eight hundred and eighty-seven *Moai* on the island,' said Carlos helpfully. 'Two hundred and eighty-eight stand on special stone platforms at various places on the coast. Some platforms have only one statue, others as many as fifteen.'

First Carlos drove us to Ranu Raraku, the main quarry, where most, though not all, of the *Moai* were carved. More *Moai*, some still unfinished, were scattered all over the bare rocky area.

Carlos reeled off more statistics.

'There are three hundred and ninety-seven *Moai* still in the quarry,' he informed us. 'And ninety-two more scattered all over the area.'

I said, 'As if they'd started their journey to the coast but just didn't make it . . .'

Carlos shrugged. 'Perhaps, *señor*. Who knows? It is all a great mystery.'

We saw the line of no less than fifteen *Moai* at Tongariki, once smashed down and scattered by the sea, now restored by devoted local archaeologists.

We saw more *Moai* at Anakena, near Hangaroa village.

The white coral eyes of the *Moai* had been

restored so that they seemed to stare above the village as if searching the skies.

Flagging by now, we stopped for a late picnic lunch on Anakena's white sand beach. Carlos had brought along a hamper, with bread, cold chicken and fruit. Plus a bottle of Chilean wine which did wonders for Dad's morale.

After lunch Carlos was keen to rush us off again.

'There is so much more to see,' he said enthusiastically. 'The restored ceremonial village at Orongo with interesting tiny houses and many fascinating rock carvings. There are cultural performances to see, with native music and dancing . . .'

Dad shuddered. 'Let's just sit here and take things in for a bit,' he said.

I nodded. 'I quite agree. I think I'm suffering from cultural overload.'

Dad took another swig of wine. 'What do you make of it all, Matthew?'

'It's weird,' I said. 'Like Carlos says, it's all a great mystery. There's something very strange about all those statues. A kind of alien quality.'

Dad gave me a quizzical look. 'Do you mean that literally?'

'I'm not sure. It's all so baffling. The natives of a tiny island, miles from anywhere, get a sudden passion for carving massive great statues of alien figures and setting them up around the coast. With the tools and resources they had, it must have taken thousands of people hundreds of years. A thousand statues – all hacked from volcanic rock with stone hammers!'

'The carving is perfectly possible,' argued Dad, 'given enough people and enough time. And even the transportation of the statues has been shown to be theoretically possible.'

'Oh, I know all about the theories,' I said. 'Rocking the statues to and fro with levers, dragging them along on rollers, floating them on rafts . . . As I remember, the archaeologists didn't get far when they tried it themselves. It took them ages to move one very small statue a very little way.'

Carlos made a contribution to the discussion. 'There is an unfinished statue in the quarry called El Gigante,' he said. 'It lies on the ground, it is twenty metres long and weighs two hundred and seventy-four tonnes. Even the archaeologists cannot suggest any way it could have been raised upright, let alone moved.'

'What does native tradition say about the statues?' I asked.

'*Mana*,' said Carlos simply. 'The gods came from the skies and gave the people *Mana*. It is said that the *Moai* moved to their appointed places by night, at the orders of the priests.'

'The *why* is as baffling as the *how*,' I went on.

Dad raised an eyebrow. 'What do you mean?'

'First they start this mad scheme,' I said. 'With or without *Mana* it's a heck of a lot of work. Then they just go off the idea. Only a third of the statues actually reach the sacred sites. The rest are left in the quarries or just get abandoned somewhere *en route*. What does native tradition say about that, Carlos?'

'They say the gods became angry, took away their *Mana* and went away themselves. One day perhaps they will forgive the people and return.'

The subject seemed to make Carlos uneasy. He began packing up the picnic things.

'If the distinguished *señores* have seen enough, shall I take them back to the hotel? If they wish I can return later to take them to a restaurant.'

'There is one more place I should like to see,' said Dad.

'At the *señor*'s command.'

'An archaeologist was killed in an accident a few days ago. A statue fell on him. I should like to visit the place where it happened. Do you know where it is?'

'I can take you to the very spot, *señor*. Many wished to visit the place where the tragedy happened. It is on a remote part of the island. It was just below a hilltop on an isolated headland. There is one of the smaller quarries on the top of the hill. It is a very long drive, *señor*. And at the end there are just a few statues, hardly worth seeing . . .'

'All the same,' said Dad. 'I think I'd like to go . . .'

Carlos drove us away from the beach. It was, as he had said, a very difficult drive, first across the island and then along winding coastal roads. Finally we reached a spot just below a conical hill on a lonely headland.

Carlos stopped the Land Rover at a bend in the road and jumped out.

He turned back towards us, an expression of bafflement on his face. '*Impossible!*' he gasped.

We got out of the Land Rover.

'What's up?' I asked.

'It was here!' said Carlos. 'The poor man was by the side of the road. The statue lay across him, and all his upper body was crushed. Now it is gone.'

'The body?'

'The body of course, *señor*. The Carabineros, the police, managed to move the statue sufficiently to free the body, and they will have taken it to their headquarters in Mataveros. In due course the poor man's body will be sent home. No, what is truly amazing is that the statue has also gone!'

Dad and I looked at each other. A statue that moved and killed was amazing enough. But a statue that disappeared afterwards . . .

'Perhaps the police moved the statue as well,' suggested Dad. 'If it was blocking the road . . .'

Carlos shook his head. 'It was at the side of the road, it was possible to drive around it. They might have moved it further to the side, though even that would have been difficult. But to take it away altogether . . .'

'You're sure this is the right place?' asked Dad. 'These bends all look much alike. Perhaps it happened somewhere further along the road?'

Once again Carlos shook his head. 'It was here, *señor*, just below that hill, I am certain.

Besides, there are still – signs.' He pointed to a dark patch at the side of the road.

Dad went and knelt by the patch and poked at it cautiously. He studied the end of his finger, sniffed it, and then wiped it with his handkerchief.

'Blood,' he confirmed. 'This is the place.'

'That means there are two mysteries,' I said. 'How did the statue leave? And, just as puzzling, how did it get here in the first place?'

We both looked at Carlos.

He pointed to the hill above us. 'That is one of the smaller quarries, on the very top of that hill. There were three *Moai* in the quarry originally, and one of them was found down here, toppled over on its side. The police believe that the dead man was making efforts to move the *Moai* – such attempts have been made before – and it rolled over on him.'

'But surely it would have rolled on him up there, in the quarry?' I said. 'How did he get himself crushed down here?'

'Perhaps our friend Abernethy can tell us,' said Dad.

I looked up and saw Professor Abernethy striding down the hillside towards us. With him was a tall, fair young man and, trailing behind, a small, dark-haired girl.

They were the two who'd met him at the airport.

Professor Abernethy swept down on us like a big, hairy thundercloud.

'Professor Stirling! What the devil are you doing here?'

It wasn't the right kind of tone to take with Dad. 'I might ask you the same question,' he said icily.

'I'm working, man! My archaeological team is excavating the quarry on top of yon hill.'

'Won't you introduce us to your colleagues, sir?' I said politely.

'This is Mike Fallon,' grunted Professor Abernethy.

The girl came hurrying up to join us. Both Abernethy and Fallon ignored her.

I went over to her and gave her a friendly smile. 'How do you do?' I said. 'I'm Matt Stirling, and this is my father, Professor James Stirling.'

'I'm Anna,' she said shyly. 'Anna Sherwood.'

We shook hands.

'How's the work going?' I asked.

'Very well. Mike found the new site – it's so

small everyone ignores it,' Anna replied. 'But we've made some very interesting discoveries . . .'

Fallon snapped, 'Anna! You know the professor doesn't like us talking about our work!'

The girl lapsed into a guilty silence.

I looked curiously at Mike Fallon and decided I didn't much like what I saw. I didn't like his film-star good looks, his bullying manner, his air of self-importance.

Fallon glared haughtily back at me. I could feel the tension coming off him in waves. It struck me that he, rather than Abernethy, was the real fanatic.

The two professors, meanwhile, were bristling at each other like two tomcats on the same wall.

'Ye still haven't answered my question,' growled Abernethy.

'What question was that?'

'What are you doing here? Why are you sticking your long nose into my excavation?'

'My dear man, I haven't been anywhere near your excavation. I'm simply being a tourist. It occurred to me to take a look at the place where this very remarkable accident took place.'

'I'm sorry to see a man of your eminence

giving way to morbid curiosity, Professor Stirling.'

'And I'm sorry to see someone of yours falling victim to paranoia, Professor Abernethy!'

Anna gasped. She was watching the exchange with horrified fascination, turning her head from one to the other like a spectator at a tennis match.

Professor Abernethy's beard bristled with rage.

'And what do you mean by that?'

'My dear man, I'm a space scientist, not a rival archaeologist out to steal your secrets.'

'Secrets?' shouted Abernethy. 'Who said anything about secrets?'

Dad finally lost it. 'Now see here, Abernethy, I don't care what tin-pot discovery you think you've made at your wretched site. I don't care if you've found the Holy Grail or proved that the inhabitants of Easter Island are one of the Lost Tribes of Israel! I'm just not interested!'

Before Professor Abernethy could explode back at him I said hurriedly, 'We *are* interested in one thing, though. How that statue got down here, and where it's got to now. Any ideas?'

The young man Fallon said, 'The police think Rankin must have weakened the area round the statue with his excavation.'

'But how did it roll over on him, down here on the road?'

'If it started to roll down the hill he might have chased it,' said Fallon. 'Tried to stop it, even.'

It was possible, I thought. Not likely, but possible.

'And where's the statue now?'

'The police took it away on a truck,' growled Professor Abernethy. 'It's down at police HQ labelled "Exhibit A". Now, if you've no more daft questions, some of us have got work to do!'

He marched off back up the hillside, Fallon close behind him.

I turned to Anna. 'Goodbye!' I said. 'Maybe we can meet again in less fraught circumstances!'

She gave me a nervous smile and hurried after the others.

We got back in the Land Rover and Carlos drove away.

'I am sorry to say your friend was lying, *señor*,' he said.

Dad frowned. 'About the police taking the statue? Surely it might be true?'

Carlos shook his head decisively. 'There are only a dozen Carabineros on the island. Even if they had the desire they do not have the ability. Besides, why would they trouble themselves? There was no doubt about the cause of death. What were they hoping to find on the *Moai*? Fingerprints?'

We drove on for a while in a thoughtful silence, following the winding road around the curve of a steeper hill.

Suddenly I heard a rumbling, grinding sound.

I looked up and saw a massive column of stone, rolling down the steep hillside towards us . . .

Chapter Four

ATTACK

The massive thing rolling down the hillside towards us was roughly cylindrical in shape.

It was moving too quickly for me to make out many details, and it was surrounded with dirt and dust thrown up by its passage.

But I knew what it was all the same.

It was one of the *Moai* – presumably the one that had killed Doctor Rankin.

Now it was after us – and it was travelling very fast.

Too fast. As if something was . . . driving it.

'Look out!' I yelled.

Even as I shouted, I felt the Land Rover surge forward. Carlos had seen the rolling statue too. He was trying to outpace it.

As the statue hurtled down the hillside towards us, I realised something else.

Carlos's plan wasn't going to work.

The statue was being *guided*.

As we sped along the coastal road the statue's angle of descent was changing to keep pace with us. When it reached the road it would smash into the Land Rover and destroy us all.

By the time all this had gone through my mind the rolling statue was almost upon us.

I leaned forward and yelled in Carlos's ear. 'Brake, Carlos! *Brake – now!'*

Carlos stood on the brakes, the Land Rover juddered to a halt – and the massive stone shape of the *Moai* flashed in front of the Land Rover's front bumper, missing us by what felt like centimetres.

It rolled across the little stretch of open ground between the road and the sea and disappeared over the edge of the cliff.

Dad and I looked at each other without speaking. Followed by Carlos we got out of the car and walked over to the cliff edge.

Far below, at the bottom of a jagged black cliff, was the statue, half-buried in white sand. It had landed on its back, and the blank eyes seemed to be staring up at us.

I shuddered.

'I doubt if it can climb cliffs,' I said hopefully.

Dad said, 'Let's not take any chances. Will

you take us back to the hotel please, Carlos?'

We were all pretty quiet on the drive back.

I think we were all shaken up, not only by what had happened to us, but by all it implied.

When we pulled up outside the hotel Dad said, 'I think we'll have dinner in the hotel tonight, Carlos.'

'Won't you join us?' I said.

Carlos looked shocked. 'That would not be fitting, señor. Do not concern yourself, I have a cousin in the hotel kitchen. I shall do very well. If you need me I will not be far away.'

He vanished round the back of the hotel.

Dad and I cleaned off the dust of travel and then sat down in the tiny sitting-room that bordered our two bedrooms. We ordered drinks from room service – a large brandy for Dad, a Coke for me.

When the waiter had gone, Dad took a large swig of brandy and said, 'Well!'

'Well, indeed!' I echoed.

I was still pretty shaken by what had happened. If I closed my eyes I could see that massive stone statue rolling towards us.

Dad was shaken too, though he was determined not to show it. 'Time to take stock,' he said, gulping down his brandy. 'For a start, should we report what happened to the police – these Carabineros Carlos mentioned?'

'Always a bit tricky, reporting the impossible,' I said. 'Do you think they'd believe us?'

'We could produce our official credentials.'

'Even so . . .'

'There's the statue on the beach to back up our story,' said Dad.

'If it's still there – it moved before, remember. Besides, if we tell the police and they launch an investigation, the news will get out and there'll be even more panic about the *Moai* moving. That's what we're here to prevent. I think we ought to go on investigating alone – at least for a while.'

Dad nodded. 'On balance, I think you're right. Very well. But where do we start? We know almost nothing about what's going on.'

'We know that the statues can move,' I said. Then I corrected myself. 'Or rather, we know that they can *be* moved – by someone or something.'

'You're sure of that?'

I shrugged. 'A statue was used to kill Rankin, and a *Moai*, probably the same one, was used to attempt to kill us.'

Dad said thoughtfully, 'Well, I suppose the

only alternative to your theory is to believe that the statues themselves are both sentient and malignant – which seems even less likely. Very well, we'll assume there's some kind of guiding intelligence behind all this. But who's doing all this? And, come to that, how?'

'The how is easier to work out than the who,' I said. 'I've got a theory . . .'

Dad put on his sceptical face. 'I sense some more of your wild ideas coming up, Matthew.'

'We're in a pretty wild situation,' I pointed out.

Dad gave one of his rare smiles. 'True. Go on.'

'We've already talked about the standard archaeological explanations for the statues,' I said. 'The rational ones, I mean.'

'Personally, I find rational explanations per-fectly adequate,' said Dad.

I grinned. Good old Dad. Even after our recent experience – all our recent experiences – he was as sceptical as ever.

'In this case they may be adequate – but they're just not convincing,' I said. 'They don't feel right.'

Dad frowned. 'I don't follow. Surely the facts . . .'

'It's the facts that bother me,' I said. 'Nearly a

thousand statues! Giant statues standing four metres and weighing fourteen tonnes or more. More than two hundred of them moved to sacred sites all over the island!' I paused. 'All right, so it *could* have been achieved by thousands of natives chipping away with little stone hammers for hundreds of years – and then moving these socking great statues on rollers or something, a few centimetres at a time for a few more hundred years . . .'

'You have some other explanation?'

'In this case the rational explanation just doesn't seem sensible. I find it much easier to believe in the existence of *Mana* – especially after today.'

'Magic? Really, Matthew.'

'No, not magic,' I said. 'TK.'

TK is short for telekinesis – the moving of physical objects by the power of the mind.

Dad frowned. 'The existence of telekinesis has never been scientifically proved . . .'

It was my turn to give him a scornful look. 'Oh come on, Dad, what about poltergeists?'

Poltergeists – it's a German word meaning noisy ghosts – are the ones who slam doors in the middle of the night, smash windows and send cups and plates flying across the room.

They're sort of supernatural hooligans, specialising in pointless and destructive mischief – and there are literally hundreds of well-documented cases.

Even Dad is prepared to admit that there's overwhelming evidence of the existence of poltergeists.

Naturally he favours the scientific rather than the supernatural explanation.

The theory is that poltergeists are really caused by a sort of involuntary TK.

In an overwhelming number of cases of poltergeist activity there's an unhappy teenager, usually, but not always, female, somewhere on the scene. The theory is that all this teenage torment unleashes the dormant powers of telekinesis in the human mind. The pointless destruction is a reflection of teenage misery.

'There's a big difference between chucking a cup and moving a *Moai*,' Dad pointed out.

'Maybe, but the principle's the same,' I said. 'If TK exists, and we've both seen evidence that it does, there may be literally no limits to its power.'

Dad was getting impatient. 'What exactly are you suggesting, Matthew?'

'Let's just suppose that some time in the past

the Easter Islanders developed *Mana* – the power of some kind of controlled TK.'

'Bestowed upon them by benevolent alien visitors from outer space, no doubt?'

'Perhaps. Or perhaps they discovered it for themselves. Maybe it was some kind of genetic freak brought on by years of isolation and inbreeding. Anyway, let's just say they acquired it somehow.'

'And used it first to make and then to move the statues?'

'Exactly. It still doesn't explain the why, but it could account for the how.'

'All right,' said Dad. 'Say I accept this fantastic theory, just for the moment. If the natives had this wonderful power, why did they suddenly abandon their plans and leave two-thirds of the statues in the quarries where they were made?'

'Because the *Mana* ran out,' I said triumphantly. 'Somehow or other they lost the power of TK. Maybe the secret was lost, maybe it just burned out, maybe the aliens took it away. Anyway, it was gone, so the grand plan was never completed.'

'Let's get back to the rational for a moment,' said Dad. 'The statue that nearly killed us *could* have been set moving by normal physical means.'

I shook my head. 'It won't wash, Dad. Look how close it came.'

'That still doesn't prove . . .'

'Imagine you're up on a hill with a boulder and you want to crush a car moving quite fast along the road below. What are your chances? The boulder will roll too slowly, the people in the car will see it coming, step on the gas and get out of the way. That statue was going like the clappers and it was chasing us. When Carlos accelerated, the statue changed its angle of approach. It was being guided!'

Dad was silent for a moment.

'All right,' he said. 'Let's say I accept your hypothesis – purely for the purposes of discussion. How does it relate to today's events?'

'Simple,' I said. 'Somebody's rediscovered the *Mana*! Suppose the power wasn't lost for good but buried somehow, hidden? Somebody gets on the track of it, revives it, starts experimenting . . . That could account for the missing and moving statues, and for the death of that archaeologist.'

'And the attack on us?'

'Whoever's discovered the lost secret doesn't want to share it with anybody. If they decided we were a threat . . .'

Dad shook his head. 'It's a worrying thought.'

'It's a lot more worrying than you realise,' I said. 'Look!'

I pointed to my open bedroom doorway. 'Come and look at my view!'

We both got up and went over to my bedroom.

Through the window you could see the line of *Moai* gazing impassively down at us. I had a sudden image of them advancing, crashing through the walls . . .

Dad nodded. 'I see what you mean. Let's hope our unknown intelligence draws the line at demolishing hotels!'

'It might not need to,' I said. 'There are nearly a thousand statues on Easter Island, remember. We'll be pretty close to some of the *Moai* wherever we go!'

We went back to the sitting-room.

Dad said, 'There's one final point we haven't really discussed, Matthew – the identity of this mysterious guiding intelligence.'

'I hate to say it,' I said, 'but there's one over-whelmingly obvious candidate.'

'Professor Abernethy?'

I nodded. 'That's right. Professor Abernethy. He was too interested in us at the airport. He delivered some kind of obscure warning when we were getting on the plane. And he was very hostile when we got near to his archaeological site. Immediately after that we were attacked.'

'I can't believe that Abernethy would try to kill me,' said Dad. 'A fellow scientist, after all . . .'

'You said yourself he was paranoid. He's obviously obsessed with Easter Island. If he's made a discovery – a really earth-shaking discovery like the existence of *Mana* and he thought you were trying to steal it . . .'

'But why should he think I was trying to steal it?' protested Dad. 'I don't even work in his field.'

'You work for the Scientific Research Institute now, remember. If he knows that he might well assume you were after the secret of *Mana*. To the paranoiac, everyone is a potential enemy.'

Dad shook his head. 'All the same, I should hate to think that Abernethy . . .' He jumped up. 'I must talk to him, have it out . . .'

'I wouldn't advise it.'

'Why ever not?'

'Because if he really is paranoid, he won't trust anything you say. He'll think it's all a cunning plan to trap him. Besides . . .'

I hesitated.

'Besides what?' snapped Dad.

'You're not the most tactful person in the world,' I said bluntly. 'And if you provoke him . . .'

I nodded towards the line of giant statues outside my window.

'I am perfectly capable of being diplomatic – what are you grinning at, Matthew?'

Before I could reply there was a tap at the door.

Dad gave me a smouldering glare and growled, 'Come in.'

The door opened, revealing Carlos.

'My apologies for this intrusion, *señores*,' he said. 'I felt I should warn you that someone is asking for you at reception.'

'Who can that be? We don't know anyone here.'

I knew the answer even before Carlos provided it.

'It is Professor Abernethy, *señor*.'

Chapter Five

ENCOUNTER

Dad and I looked at each other for a moment.

Dad said, 'Well, since he's here . . .'

I nodded. 'Would you mind bringing him over, Carlos? And please – stay with us when he arrives.'

'With pleasure, *señor*.'

Carlos faded away.

Dad gave me an enquiring look.

I shrugged. 'There's something very reassuring about Carlos. Besides, I thought it might be useful to have a witness.'

We waited in silence for a few minutes. Then the door opened again. Carlos showed Professor Abernethy into the room, and remained standing by the door.

Dad made an effort to be diplomatic.

'Ah, Professor Abernethy, how nice to see you. Can I offer you a drink?'

'No, nothing, thank you.' Abernethy glared

suspiciously around the room. 'I was hoping for a few words in private.'

'You already know my son Matthew,' said Dad. 'Carlos is our guide – and our friend. Anything you have to say you can say in front of them both.'

'As you wish.'

Dad waved Abernethy to a seat and we all sat down.

All except Carlos, who remained standing by the door.

Professor Abernethy seemed to find it hard to begin.

'I was a wee bit terse when we met earlier,' he muttered. 'I'm thinking I maybe owe you an apology.'

I could see Dad was about to say something like 'You most certainly do!' so I hurriedly intervened.

'That's all right,' I said. 'Think nothing of it.'

Abernethy said, 'Some odd things have been happening around that site. Poor Rankin was killed. I didn't want anyone else to get hurt. I was concerned for your safety.'

'Not without reason,' said Dad drily. 'Soon after we left you we were attacked and nearly killed ourselves.'

'Attacked? Who by?'

'By a moving statue,' I said. 'Just like Doctor Rankin.'

'What? Kindly explain yourself, boy!'

Dad gave him a brief account of what had happened.

Abernethy listened in what seemed like genuine astonishment. 'That's terrible, man, terrible!' he said. 'It's unbelievable.'

'Is it?' said Dad. 'As Matthew says, something very similar seems to have happened to your colleague Rankin.'

'Aye, that it did,' said Abernethy. 'You see now, I was right to be concerned. For your own safety, stay away from that site!'

The strange thing was that he seemed to be quite sincere.

'Have you any idea what's causing the trouble?' I asked.

'I've an idea that the site is more important, more sacred than we ever realised,' said Abernethy. 'It's possible that some of the Rapanui – the native islanders, ye ken – resent our interference. That's why they killed Rankin.'

'Why would anyone attack *us*?' asked Dad.

'When they saw us talking earlier, they

maybe thought you were colleagues of mine, more off-island archaeologists come to pry into their secrets.'

'It sounds as if you're the one who needs to be careful,' said Dad. 'Hadn't you better abandon your work on the site before someone else gets hurt?'

'It's no' that simple,' growled Abernethy. 'Things have gone too far. I have to stay, I've got responsibilities to the rest of my team – and to science as well. It's possible I can still sort things out – but I don't want to have to worry about you two while I'm doing it.'

'There must be an awful lot of these angry islanders,' I said.

Abernethy glared at me. 'What do you mean, boy?'

'If they can chuck statues at people who annoy them – and take them away afterwards.'

I saw from Abernethy's face that I'd struck a chord.

He knew, or at least suspected, that the *Moai* were being moved by something other than brute force.

Abernethy stood up. 'Well, I've done my best for you both. If you won't listen, you won't. You'd do well to leave the island just as soon as you can.'

'It's not just a matter of not listening,' said Dad. 'I fail to see why I should interrupt my holiday . . .'

'Holiday be damned,' growled Abernethy. 'I know all about this fine new job of yours, Stirling. Paranormal research, indeed! Well don't try to do any of your paranormal research around my site. You'll find it isn't safe!'

There was a knock on the door and Carlos opened it. 'Two more visitors, *señor*,' he announced cheerfully.

Mike Fallon and Anna Sherwood came into the room.

'Professor Abernethy!' said Anna. 'Are you all right?'

'Why wouldn't I be all right?'

Fallon said, 'You seemed – disturbed, this afternoon. When you jumped in the station wagon and rushed off here – well, we thought we'd better follow you.'

'You'd do better to mind your own damned business!'

The two glared angrily at each other. It struck me that relations on Abernethy's archaeological team weren't all that wonderful.

Dad wasn't too pleased at being invaded by archaeologists. Apart from anything else, our little sitting-room was getting uncomfortably crowded.

'It seems to be my day for visitors,' he said. 'Won't you introduce your two colleagues, Professor Abernethy?'

'I told you their names before . . .'

'And I'm afraid I've forgotten them. Be so good as to tell me again.'

'Anna Sherwood, Mike Fallon,' said Abernethy grumpily.

'I'm Professor Stirling. This is my son Matthew, and that's Carlos, our guide.'

I looked thoughtfully at Abernethy's two assistants.

I couldn't help noticing that Anna was very pretty – and not all that much older than me.

Not that I had much hope of making an impression there.

Fallon was tall and fair with one of those classical profiles – the Greek god type.

It was quite clear from the way Anna looked at him she thought he was wonderful – and equally clear from his general manner that he agreed with her.

Ignoring everyone else, Fallon spoke directly

to Abernethy. 'There's still a good deal of work to be done on the site, professor . . .'

'If you're meaning tonight's excavation, I was wanting to discuss that with you. I dinna see why . . .'

'Perhaps we should talk in private, professor,' said Fallon with a meaningful glance at the rest of us. 'We don't want to bore Professor Stirling with our affairs.'

Dad and I looked at each other. Whatever was going on at that site, it was quite clear that Fallon was even more paranoid about it than Abernethy himself.

'Aye, verra well,' growled Abernethy. 'We can talk on the way back to the site.'

He stomped out of the room without any attempt at a farewell, and Fallon followed him.

Dad went to the door and called after them. 'Thank you for a most interesting discussion, Professor Abernethy. I'll think over all you've said.'

The girl Anna gave us an apologetic look. 'I'm sorry about all this. They're not usually so rude. But work on the site's reached a critical stage, and with all this trouble . . . Everyone's pretty tense.'

'That's all right,' I said. 'Look, can't you stay and talk for a while?'

'I really must be getting back.'

I followed her to the door and we went round to the front of the hotel. Fallon and Abernethy were climbing into a battered old station wagon.

'Come along, Anna!' called Fallon.

Suddenly Abernethy said, 'I think you'd better stay here, Anna. We'll no' be needing you tonight. You can get a taxi back to the cottage.'

Fallon said, 'Professor, I really think Anna ought to . . .'

Ignoring him, Abernethy put the station wagon into gear and screeched away.

Anna looked after them with an expression of comical dismay. 'They've left me behind!'

'Didn't you and Fallon have a car – as well as the professor, I mean?' I asked.

She shook her head. 'No, there's only one car, and Professor Abernethy took that when he said he had to come here and see you. After a while Mike got worried and insisted we come after him. We walked for a bit and then hitched a lift on a tourist coach.'

She looked worriedly after the disappearing station wagon. 'I don't want to go back to the cottage. I want to be at the site for tonight's excavation. You heard Mike, he wants me to be there . . .'

Dad and Carlos had come up to join us.

'My dear young lady, we'll be delighted to drive you wherever you want to go,' said Dad. 'Won't we, Carlos?'

'It will be an honour, *señorita*.'

'On one condition,' Dad went on. 'That you stay and have dinner with us first.'

I looked at him in amazement. The old boy was oozing charm in a way that was quite unlike himself. For a moment I thought he must be smitten with Anna. Then I realised. He saw her as a source of information – and a way of getting back to that site.

'Do stay,' I said. 'You're entitled to eat, after all, and we'll take you back to the site afterwards.'

She looked at her watch. 'I suppose I could. The excavation doesn't start till later. All right, thank you, I accept.' She smiled for the first time. 'To tell you the truth, it will be a relief to get away for a while!'

As we headed for the hotel, I was wondering why Abernethy had wanted to leave Anna behind.

Perhaps he was concerned for her safety . . .

Over what turned out to be a surprisingly good dinner we learned quite a lot about affairs on Professor Abernethy's site. We didn't have to interrogate Anna either. She was eager to talk, and it all came pouring out.

As I'd suspected, she was one of Abernethy's students, and although she didn't say so, she'd obviously joined the dig largely because she had a crush on Fallon.

There had been tensions on the site from the start.

Fallon was a graduate student, Abernethy's favourite – until he began challenging Abernethy's authority.

'It was only natural in a way,' she said loyally. 'It was Mike who discovered the new site – or at least, he discovered how important it was.'

Apparently Fallon was an expert on Rapanui folklore, and his researches had led him to believe that this lonely hillside site, regarded up till now as being of little interest, was really the most important of all.

'Then Professor Abernethy had to go back to England to raise more funding. While he was away, Mike spent more and more time on the new site, working on his own. Eventually he persuaded Rankin to change from the site Abernethy had chosen to the one he'd discovered.'

'Rankin had been left in charge?' I asked.

She smiled. 'He was supposed to be. But Mike can be very forceful – and poor little Rankin was rather easily led.'

'What happened next?' I asked.

'After we'd worked on the site for a while, Rankin seemed to get cold feet. Apparently there had been protests from the Rapanui community. Some kind of priest appeared, and warned us to leave the site alone. Rankin was worried about what Abernethy would say when he got back. He wanted to switch back to Abernethy's original site. He and Mike were still arguing about it when there was that terrible accident.'

'Were you there when it happened?' asked Dad.

She shook her head. 'I was away in town, buying provisions. Mike said Rankin had some theory about the way the statues were moved. He was trying to move one of the statues down the hill to the cliff edge when it tipped over and rolled on him . . .'

It didn't sound all that convincing to me. But

then, love is blind. It was quite clear that Anna was prepared to believe anything that Fallon told her.

'I imagine Professor Abernethy wasn't best pleased when he got back,' said Dad.

'He was furious,' said Anna simply. 'He and Mike had the most terrible row. Abernethy wanted to go back to the original site, but Mike persuaded him to agree that that we could work on the new site for just a little longer. He said he could prove how important it was.'

'Did he say how?' I asked.

'It's all tied up with this dig tonight,' said Anna.

'Why so late?' asked Dad.

'Mike insisted we open the mound at moon-rise. Apparently there's a full moon.'

'What mound?' asked Dad keenly.

'There's a mound in the centre of the circle of statues. Mike insists it's a burial mound. Apparently it's some kind of Rapanui festival tonight and Mike said that tonight at moonrise was the appointed time – whatever that means.'

'What's Abernethy's attitude to all this?'

'Initially he was sort of half-angry, half-amused. He's quite fond of Mike really – Mike was always his star pupil. Professor Abernethy said he'd humour Mike for tonight, but tomorrow we return to the proper dig. But I think now he's a bit anxious about Mike . . .'

'What do you think Mike's up to?' I asked.

'I'm not sure. But he said tonight was all he needed. After tonight everyone would know he was right.' She looked at her watch. 'Thanks for a lovely meal but I'd really better get back. It can't be very long until moonrise and I want to be there for the dig . . .'

It was getting dark when we came out of the hotel. Dark and hot and humid – somehow the air seemed tense with electricity.

Carlos stood waiting by the Land Rover, and I handed Anna into the back seat.

'I'm sorry to ask you to work so late, Carlos,' said Dad. 'This young lady needs to get back to her friends. They're on the hill site where we were this afternoon.'

'Then undoubtedly we must take her there,' said Carlos.

'I think I ought to warn you it may be dangerous,' I said.

'Do not worry, *señor*, I am prepared.'

With amazing suddenness, Carlos produced

the most enormous revolver I've ever seen from somewhere underneath his crumpled linen jacket. Just as suddenly the weapon disappeared.

I looked at him in astonishment. 'Carlos, you're full of surprises!' I said.

'What on earth are you doing with a revolver?' demanded Dad.

'It is my duty to protect my clients,' said Carlos loftily. 'It is all part of the service, professor!'

I got in the back beside Anna, Dad got in the front with Carlos and we drove away, down the winding coastal road, past the black cliffs holding back the stormy sea, towards the lonely headland hillside where the statues stood waiting for us . . .

Chapter Six

RETURN

We were all pretty quiet on the ride out to the site.

Anna was looking worried, Dad looked grave, and I was feeling pretty grim myself.

I was wondering if we ought to go out to the site at all.

We certainly wouldn't be welcome. If my ideas were correct, we'd be in a good deal of danger.

But then, there didn't seem to be much choice.

Anna would insist on going, whether we drove her out there or not, and it was out of the question to let her go alone.

Besides which, events seemed to be coming to some kind of climax. I'd formed a rough sort of theory about what was going on and I desperately wanted to *know*.

That was my real motive, I thought. Curiosity. I knew Dad must feel the same. It was one of the things we had in common.

I remembered one of Mum's old sayings when I was little, and always asking questions: 'Curiosity killed the cat.'

I just hoped curiosity wasn't going to get us all killed.

Calm and cheerful as ever, Carlos drove us through the warm, flower-scented night.

We were driving along the winding coastal road when Dad said, 'I'm not too happy about this trip, Matthew.'

'Me neither.'

'You saw the state Professor Abernethy was in. There's no telling what he might do.'

'Or what someone might do to him,' I said.

Anna looked alarmed. 'Why should anyone harm the professor?'

'For talking to us,' I said. 'You'd better be careful as well. Better stay close to us.'

Soon after that we saw the conical hill looming up on the skyline.

Anna said, 'We can only drive as far as the base of the hill. There's a kind of track . . .'

'Don't drive too close, Carlos,' said Dad quietly. 'I'd like to approach unobserved if we can.'

Carlos drove off the road and parked the car

on a patch of open ground, some little way from the bottom of the hill.

We all climbed out.

You could just see the beginning of the rough track leading up to the hilltop.

'Look!' said Anna and pointed upwards.

The full moon was rising over the hill.

Suddenly we heard pounding footsteps and deep, rasping breaths.

Someone was running down the track.

Someone in fear of his life.

A shape emerged from the darkness and stumbled towards us.

It was Professor Abernethy. He was dishevelled and grimy and there was a smear of blood on his forehead.

'It moved!' he gasped. 'It moved . . .'

'Professor, what's happened?' called Anna. 'What moved?'

I had a terrible feeling that I already knew the answer.

Moments later we saw for ourselves.

One of the statues, a *Moai*, loomed up out of the darkness.

It wasn't rolling, like the one that had come after us. It was upright, gliding smoothly across the rough ground, as if suspended by some invisible force.

It was chasing Professor Abernethy.

Gasping and exhausted Abernethy looked over his shoulder – and saw the great statue bearing down on him.

He stopped, frozen in horror.

Moving in ghastly silence the statue rushed towards him like a train.

Suddenly I found I was up and running.

I pounded towards Abernethy, tackled him low, and barged him out of the statue's path.

We collapsed in a heap together, and I felt the wind of the statue's passage as it hurtled by us.

'Down!' I yelled. 'Nobody move!'

Abernethy lay motionless beneath me and for a long moment everything was silent and still.

I felt rather than saw the statue glide past me again as it headed back towards the hill.

Moments later I raised my head. The *Moai* was nowhere to be seen. Slowly and cautiously I got to my feet.

Abernethy lay quite still, staring white-faced and wide-eyed at the sky, where the full moon was emerging from behind black clouds. For a moment I thought he was dead.

I crouched beside him and saw with relief that he was breathing shallowly. I tried to find a pulse in his neck, but the mass of straggly whiskers made it difficult to locate.

A voice behind me said quietly, 'All right, Matthew, let me.'

Dad had come over from the Land Rover.

Thankfully I left the job to him. There's a seldom-used medical degree amongst his mass of qualifications.

As I got up I saw Anna and Carlos approaching.

Carlos had his revolver in his hand.

Before anyone could speak I put a finger to my lips. 'Speak quietly, and make as little noise as you can,' I whispered. 'I think that thing may home in on noise and movement. We don't want to attract it back.'

Everyone moved and spoke very quietly after that.

Anna looked down at Professor Abernethy. 'He's not dead, is he?'

Dad got to his feet and shook his head. 'He's in shock.'

'Shouldn't we get him to a hospital?'

'Soon, yes, but he's in no immediate danger.'

'No more than the rest of us,' I said.

Dad said, 'I need to find out what's happening up at that site. I suggest the rest of you wait down here.'

'Forget it,' I said. 'I want to know what's happening as well.'

Anna said, 'I'm coming too, it concerns me more than anyone.'

'I also,' said Carlos. He smiled. 'I think it will be more frightening to wait here alone than to come!'

Dad said, 'I really think . . .'

'There's no time to argue, Dad,' I said. 'The moon's up – we don't want to miss everything.'

He nodded, accepting the situation.

'What about the professor?' asked Anna. 'We can't just leave him lying here on the ground.'

'We'd better get him into the Land Rover,' said Dad.

Even with four of us, shifting someone of Abernethy's size was no joke. He was still completely unconscious, a dead-weight. We lugged him across to the Land Rover and settled him as well as we could in the big back seat. Carlos produced a blanket and tucked it round him.

'He'll do for the moment,' said Dad. 'All right, let's go.'

We set off for the hill.

When we reached the bottom Anna said, 'Better let me lead the way, I know the path.'

We began to climb.

We moved up the steep, rocky path in single file; Anna first, then Dad, then me, with Carlos bringing up the rear.

Moonlight gleamed on the black, shiny rocks, and I suddenly realised that the little hill must be volcanic in origin.

We were climbing up to the summit of a dead volcano.

At least, I hoped it was dead.

I had a feeling that something was alive up there.

When we were nearly at the top Anna stopped and whispered, 'The last bit of the path goes into a kind of gully. At the end of the gully there's a hollow at the top of the hill with a mound in the middle.'

We followed her along the path and into the gully.

It broadened out at the end as she'd said, leading into a steep-sided bowl with a low mound in the centre.

It occurred to me that none of this could be seen unless you actually climbed the hill.

Maybe that, combined with its isolated position, was why the little site had remained so obscure.

From a distance, or even from quite close, the little hill would look like just another volcanic outcrop, a low conical hill with the top sliced off.

The reality was very different.

For a start the black hollow had a definite atmosphere.

It was, quite clearly, a place of power.

Three statues were grouped in a semi-circle on the far side of the central mound.

Standing before them was an extraordinary figure.

It wore a narrow leather loincloth and an elaborate headdress, and carried a ceremonial spear. I had seen pictures of similar costumes worn by native islanders during their religious ceremonies.

But this was no Rapanui high priest.

This was Fallon.

I had to admit he made a splendid, barbaric figure in the native costume, his muscled body gleaming in the moonlight.

Anna was pretty impressed as well.

She ran towards him.

'Mike! What's happening? What are you doing?'

He held up a hand to warn her off. 'Back!' he roared. 'Do not dare to approach me! I am no longer the one you knew as Michael Fallon. I am Tangata Manu, the sacred birdman, ruler of the Rapanui.'

Potty, I thought. Completely potty!

Dad seemed to agree.

'Mr Fallon,' he called. 'You're not well. Come with us and we'll help you!'

'I need no one's help!' screamed Fallon. 'I have power over the *Moai*!'

He raised his hand and all three statues glided forward.

There was the sudden crack of a revolver as Carlos fired again and again, not at the statues, but – incredibly – at Fallon.

Anna screamed and we froze. But nothing happened.

Fallon threw back his head and laughed.

I looked at Carlos. 'Did you miss?'

'At this range? Each one of those shots should have killed him. He is – protected.'

Fallon held up his hand and the statues ceased their advance.

We all froze.

'You shall witness my divine greatness before you die!' shouted Fallon. 'Now I shall summon the One Who Sleeps. With his power I shall rule this island – and then the world.'

'Mike, please!' called Anna.

He ignored her.

He stretched out his hand towards the mound and it began to glow. Slowly, very slowly, a figure materialised.

It was like, and yet unlike the *Moai*.

Somehow I was quite sure it was one of the alien originals of the statues that covered the island.

It had the same thick-set body, the same long, sad face with the great nose and the jutting jaw.

As with many of the statues its long, slender hands were folded across its breast.

The main difference was its size. It was very little larger than a man. It struck me that the islanders had reproduced their alien visitors as giants simply in tribute to their power.

It looked around the dome, at the three statues, at the four of us, and finally at Fallon.

'Give me your power, Great One!' screamed Fallon. 'It is time!'

The alien stared impassively at him.

I had made contact with aliens before and perhaps my mind had been sensitised in some way.

Whatever the reason, I suddenly found myself picking up some kind of emotion.

Suddenly I realised. It was doubt.

I had communicated with aliens before. Perhaps I could do it again.

I stepped forward and shouted, 'Don't listen to him!'

The alien turned its gaze towards me and I felt, once again, the indescribable yet unmistakeable sensation – the touch of an alien mind.

I spoke to it again, concentrating hard, forming each word clearly in my mind.

'I don't know who you are, or why you're here, but this man forms no part of your plans. He's not one of the Rapanui, he's an outsider. He wants your power for his own selfish ends. He's already used it to kill those who opposed him. He is unbalanced, evil, not fit to hold your power.'

'Destroy him!' screamed Fallon. 'Destroy all the blasphemers.'

Ignoring him, the alien studied me for a moment longer. Then it unfolded its arms and stretched out a long hand, pointing towards the head of the nearest statue.

Folding its arms again it faded slowly away, seeming to merge back into the mound.

'You see?' screamed Fallon. 'The power is mine. Now I shall destroy you all!'

He stretched out his hands and the three statues began to move.

For a moment I thought we were doomed – we'd never escape all three of them.

Then I realised – the statues weren't moving towards us.

They were advancing on Fallon.

Inexorably they closed in, surrounding him, until he disappeared behind the three towering stone figures.

There came a sudden, terrible scream.

The three statues glided back to their places, leaving a crushed and broken body huddled upon the ground.

'Mike!' screamed Anna.

She tried to go towards him, but Dad grabbed her arm. 'Please, wait.'

He went over to the body, examined it briefly and then came back to us.

'I'm sorry, but he's beyond anyone's help

now. We'd better go while we can.'

    'We can't just leave him!'

    'We must,' I said.

    We made our way back down the path.

Chapter Seven

DEPARTURE

Considering all that had happened, there was surprisingly little fuss afterwards.

When we got back to the Land Rover, Professor Abernethy seemed to be in some kind of coma.

'He's still in shock,' said Dad.

'We must take him to the hospital at Hangaroa,' said Carlos.

'Will they take him in?' I asked.

'Assuredly,' said Carlos. 'I have a cousin on the medical staff.'

Anna sobbed quietly as we drove to the hospital.

'Poor Mike,' she said. 'He wasn't as confident as he looked, you know. He was nervous, highly-strung. He was desperate to be somebody, to impress Professor Abernethy and everyone else . . .'

I'd hardly known Fallon, and the little I'd

seen of him I hadn't much liked. All the same, I was glad there was someone who cared about him, someone to mourn his terrible death.

When we arrived at the little hospital, the doctor confirmed Dad's diagnosis.

Professor Abernethy had started to recover consciousness by the time we left, though he was still dazed and confused.

Not surprisingly, Anna was in a pretty bad way as well. Dad took the doctor aside and explained that, like Abernethy, she'd just seen a close friend killed in a terrible accident. The doctor promised to look after her.

Curiously, he didn't ask any questions.

I suspected he was another of Carlos's cousins . . .

We left them both there and Carlos drove us back to our hotel.

'Now I suppose we must try and explain things to the police,' said Dad when we arrived. 'Shall I try to get them on the telephone, Carlos, or would it be better to go straight to their HQ?' He sighed. 'In any case, I expect we'll be kept up all night making statements. They'll want us to go back to the site.'

'I hope not,' I said, shuddering.

I didn't want to see what the *Moai* had left of Fallon. Not again.

'If the distinguished *señor* permits, I will take care of everything,' said Carlos. 'I also have a cousin in the Carabineros.'

Dad tried to argue. 'Carlos, we can't possibly expect you . . .'

Carlos was firm with him. 'Believe me, *señor*, it is better this way. The police will not want any scandal, especially one involving two such distinguished visitors. Such things are bad for tourism, and tourism is very important to our little island.'

'Just leave it all to Carlos, Dad,' I said wearily. 'Something tells me he knows what he's doing.'

'The *señor* Matthew is wise beyond his years,' said Carlos. He looked shrewdly at us both. 'Might I ask if, in the opinion of the *señores*, the recent problems are now at an end?'

'I hope so,' said Dad. 'I'm not entirely clear exactly what's been going on here, but in my opinion it's probably over and done with, at least for the time being. Matthew?'

'I think so,' I said. 'Fallon was at the bottom of all the trouble and with him out of the way . . . I don't imagine Abernethy and Anna will be any problem. They'll probably want to leave Easter

Island as soon as they've recovered.'

Carlos said, 'Might I suggest, *señores*, that you too leave the island? There is a plane tomorrow. It will be easier to keep your names out of things if you are not actually here.'

Dad frowned. He hates being told what to do.

'My dear Carlos, I really don't think that will be possible. I'm still not convinced that we won't be involved in official enquiries into Abernethy's accident and Fallon's death. Moreover, the planes are invariably fully booked and we don't have a reservation . . .'

'Believe me, *señor*, to leave tomorrow is best,' said Carlos soothingly. 'Trust me, there will be no problems with the Carabineros. And as for the matter of the plane reservations . . .'

'I know,' I said. 'You've got a cousin with the airline!'

Eventually Dad agreed to leave next day, subject to no police objections and the plane reservations being confirmed.

Before he left, Carlos said apologetically that he might not be free to take us to the airport.

'I shall be a little occupied with arrangements,' he said. 'However, I will arrange for a taxi driver to pick you up in good time, a most reliable man.'

'Another cousin, no doubt,' said Dad acidly.

'You'll come and say goodbye before we leave, won't you, Carlos?' I said.

Carlos bowed and smiled. 'I shall do myself the honour of presenting myself at the airport to make my farewells to the distinguished *señores*.'

With that he faded away in typical Carlos fashion.

Dad and I headed back to our bungalow. It was clear he was still feeling resentful about the way Carlos had taken charge.

'He's a good little fellow, that Carlos, and one has to admit that he's been very helpful. All the same, he takes a good deal upon himself for a mere guide.'

I grinned. 'Believe me, Dad, there's nothing mere about Carlos!'

Back in our bungalow we ordered a last drink and some sandwiches before bed.

When the waiter had left Dad said, 'Well, Matthew?'

'Well what?' I said innocently.

'You're the one with all the theories. I should welcome your account of what you think has been going on.'

I took a bite of ham sandwich and washed it down with a swig of Coke.

'All right, but I warn you, theories are all I've got. And there are lots of gaps.'

'Even so . . .'

'Well, let's stick with my original wild theory,' I said.

Dad frowned. 'That aliens visited Rapanui years ago, and gave the natives some kind of power?'

I nodded. '*Mana*, TK, call it what you like. They left, and something went wrong, or something went wrong and they left, who knows? What we do know is that the natives started making statues of them, giant ones to emphasise their power. Then they started setting them up on special sites.'

'Maybe it was an attempt to get the aliens to come back,' suggested Dad.

I felt I was beginning to win him over.

'If that's what it was, it didn't work and they gave up, or maybe the *Mana* wore out. Perhaps they just lost the secret of it. Anyway, they packed it all in, leaving Easter Island in the state it's in today. Lots of statues left in the quarries but relatively few set up.'

Dad said, 'But the aliens didn't really leave – not entirely.'

'That's right. They left someone – something – behind, buried inside that hill. A beacon, a relay, in case they wanted to communicate or even come back. Whatever it was, it was a source of power – and Fallon stumbled on to it.'

'How?'

I shrugged. 'Once again, who knows? I warned you there were gaps. Perhaps Fallon learned some secret from studying the ancient rituals. Perhaps he was some kind of sensitive. Maybe he felt the alien power from the mound, began to experiment with it, to use it.'

'To move the statues, just like the islanders years before?' said Dad.

'Apparently. He started to use the statues as a weapon. When Doctor Rankin wanted to pull out, and threatened to tell Abernethy what was going on, Fallon must have used one of the *Moai* to kill him. He tried to kill us when he thought we were snooping, and again to kill Abernethy when he thought he'd been talking to us. He was mad by then, of course. I think the use of the alien power had destroyed his mind.'

'Poor old Abernethy,' said Dad. 'I misjudged

him completely. I thought he was behind it all. Instead he suspected what Fallon was up to and was trying to stop him. He really was worried about our safety.'

'Professor Abernethy was lucky,' I said. 'We all were. Lucky there was only one death.'

'Two if you count Fallon,' said Dad. He paused. 'And whatever was under that mound is still there.'

'Still there but dormant,' I said. 'It hasn't bothered anyone for hundreds of years. There's no reason why it should do so again. Unless another Fallon comes along, of course. Or the aliens return . . .'

We got to the airport early next day, checked at the ticket desk and found that our reservations were waiting for us. We were having a drink in the tiny airport bar when Dad had a sudden thought.

'What about that Chilean Secret Service chap, Santera, who was supposed to be here to help us?'

'What indeed?' I said.

Dad laughed. 'Well, I knew we couldn't expect much from a Latin American James Bond. He's probably still sitting in some secluded bar in

Santiago, playing the guitar and serenading a beautiful *señorita.*'

Suddenly there was somebody standing beside our table. It was Carlos, who'd appeared out of nowhere as usual.

But it was a very different Carlos. Instead of tattered jeans and a crumpled T-shirt he wore an immaculate white tropical suit. His hair was trimmed and he was clean-shaven except for a neat moustache.

'There you are, Carlos!' I said. 'Sit down and have a farewell drink with us. And don't tell me it wouldn't be fitting!'

'It will be an honour, *señor,*' said Carlos. 'Permit me!'

He sat down at the table and snapped his fingers. A waiter appeared, and Carlos ordered champagne.

Dad blinked, taking in Carlos's changed appearance. 'You shouldn't have got dressed up just for us,' he said.

For a genius, Dad can be very dim at times.

Carlos bowed. 'How could I wear anything but my humble best to say goodbye to my most distinguished clients?'

Suddenly Dad shouted, 'Clients! Good grief,

Carlos! We haven't paid you! Don't you realise? We haven't paid you anything at all! Not for the car hire, not for all your time, not for everything you've done for us, the dangers you've faced! Work out what we owe you at your usual rates – and then double it.' He reached for his wallet. 'No – triple it!'

Carlos looked pained. 'Please, *señor*, do not insult me. How can there be any question of money between us? Are we not friends, comrades in arms? Have we not faced death together?'

'Yes, of course, but, my dear chap, you can't possibly . . .'

It's not often you see Dad at a loss for words.

I caught Carlos's eye and we both burst out laughing.

'I really must drop this guide act,' said Carlos. But this time he spoke in a crisp, very proper English accent. 'I'm afraid it's beginning to get a grip on me!'

Dad sat in stunned silence while the waiter arrived with the champagne, opened it and poured three glasses. The penny dropped at last and he said, 'Then you must be . . .'

'Colonel Carlos Santera, Chilean Intelligence,' said Carlos. 'There is no charge for my

services, Professor Stirling. They come with the compliments of the Chilean Government.'

'Are you leaving the island with us?' I asked.

He nodded. 'I shall accompany you to Santiago, where we will report to my superiors.' Carlos smiled. 'While we are there, professor, I can show you several secluded bars and any number of attractive *señoritas*. But reluctant as I am to disappoint you, I cannot play the guitar!'

I looked at Dad. It's the first time I've ever seen the old devil blush.

'You knew, Matthew!' he said accusingly.

'I had my suspicions,' I admitted. 'Not even the most conscientious of tourist guides picks his own clients, works day and night for nothing, carries a gun, risks his life for his clients and fixes hospital beds, police enquiries and plane reservations with a snap of his fingers! Besides, he made one small slip.'

Carlos looked worried. 'I did?'

'You called Dad "professor" – before anyone told you that was his title.'

'It could have been on the luggage labels . . .'

'But it wasn't!'

Once he'd got over his shock, Dad came through like a gent.

Raising his glass he said, 'Colonel Santera, I offer you my full apologies for any disparaging remarks. It has been an honour to work with you, sir.'

'And for me to work with you, professor. And you, Matthew!'

I took a token sip of champagne and we drank our toasts. I ordered a Coke, Dad and Carlos polished off the bottle, and we all went to catch the plane.

We flew to Santiago and reported to Carlos's superiors.

They told us that Fallon's death would be classified as just one more unfortunate accident. The sacred site on the hill would be cordoned off, forbidden to tourists, archaeologists and anyone else.

From now on the One Who Sleeps could sleep on undisturbed.

Then we flew back to London and reported to Ms Alexander.

She blushed when I told her Carlos Santera sent his love.

Maybe I hadn't been so wrong about the Latin lover after all.

We wrote our report for the institute and that was that.

One more thing.

It occurs to me that perhaps I haven't been entirely fair to Easter Island.

After all, our stay was too short, too fraught and just too busy to appreciate it properly.

It's a warm and friendly place with warm, friendly people.

The climate is mild and the scenery is spectacular.

And of course, the Easter Island statues are unique.

But I don't think I want to see them again.

Whatever sleeps under the mound on the lonely hill is still there.

One day, perhaps it will awaken.

I have no idea what its purpose is, or what the aliens may have planned.

Maybe the aliens will return and the giant statues, the *Moai*, will be on the move again.

I'd just as soon not be there when it happens . . .